FURRY TAILS
The Adventures of Mr. Mackie

Written by
Staci Capehart

Illustrated by
Christy Amundson

AuthorHouse™
1663 Liberty Drive
Bloomington, IN 47403
www.authorhouse.com
Phone: 833-262-8899

Because of the dynamic nature of the Internet, any web addresses or links contained in this book may have changed since publication and may no longer be valid. The views expressed in this work are solely those of the author and do not necessarily reflect the views of the publisher, and the publisher hereby disclaims any responsibility for them.

This book is printed on acid-free paper.

ISBN: 978-1-4343-6974-1 (sc)
ISBN: 978-1-4918-6471-5 (e)

Print information available on the last page.

Published by AuthorHouse 02/26/2022

authorHOUSE®

Mr. Mackie
and the Heavenly Dog Choir

It was a glorious day the day Mr. Mackie, a most adorable and loveable snow-white Maltese, entered the gates of heaven.

A beautiful angel with long brown hair greeted him there and spread her angel wings around him with the most loving embrace. "Hi, Mr. Mackie. My name is Nita, and I've come to show you around your new home."

Mr. Mackie gazed around at his beautiful surroundings and exclaimed, "Heaven is so big and bright! I was so sad to leave my human mom on earth, but … but," he stammered, "I feel so much love here that I can't feel sad."

"That's right," said Angel Nita. "There is only love and happiness here. Once you are more familiar with your surroundings, you will discover all the neat things you can do here and you'll be just fine. Now come along, sweet dog, and I'll introduce you to some special furry people."

Mackie followed Angel Nita through the golden streets of heaven. They passed many people and beautiful buildings made of bright-colored stones. As they walked down the golden streets, everyone smiled and waved at him. "Welcome, Mr. Mackie, welcome home."

After a while, they came to a beautiful meadow. It had lush green grass and a crystal-clear lake. It was the prettiest thing he had ever seen.

"This is Dogdom, a part of God's Kingdom of Heaven," said Angel Nita. "Anything and everything your little heart desires is here for you; you are free to roam wherever and whenever you like. I know you'll be very happy here with all of your doggie friends."

Mackie stood in awe at the sights he was seeing. Dogs of all shapes and sizes were frolicking about. A big shepherd mix was chasing butterflies around and around, while a long-haired collie just rested and soaked up the warm sunshine. A little Pomeranian giggled and watched.

A perky little Maltese just like him was making her way toward him. *She looks familiar,* he thought.

Suddenly her walk turned into a run and … wham! Mackie landed upside down on the ground.

"Mackie, Mackie," she exclaimed, "it's me, Precious!"

"Wow!" Mr. Mackie said as he popped up from the ground and shook himself off. "Great to see you, ol' girl. You look terrific!"

"So do you, Mackie," Precious gushed. "Welcome to heaven!"

As the two old friends made their way around Dogdom, Precious introduced him to her furry friends. "The little Pomeranian is Muffy One.

"Yap, yap!" greeted Muffy.

Mr. Mackie recognized the shepherd mix. "Hi, Sarg," said Mackie.

"Hi, brother," Sarg responded. "This is Rachel."

The beautiful collie stood up from sunning herself and greeted Mackie with a wet lick on the side of his head. "Welcome home, Mackie," Rachel said.

"We've been waiting for you. Precious is ready to put her soprano voice to work; we've got the hymnals and we're all ready to start practicing our singing."

"Hymnals? Singing? … Uh … huh?" Mackie stammered.

Rachel looked at Precious.

Precious looked at Muffy One.

Muffy One decided to stay out of the mix and ran off after a butterfly.

Sarg finally spoke up. "Well, Mackie, it's like this: a few of us pups up here really enjoy music and singing. So we thought it would be a great idea to put a choir together and perform for all of the special souls here. We voted and elected you our choir director."

"Me … why me? I mean, I'm honored that you thought of me. But really, I don't have any experience at that sort of thing and I'm really not much of a singer."

"Precisely," said Rachel. "No offense about the singing, Mr. Mackie, but you have a talent for organizing, as well as a knack for helping others."

Sarg piped in, "What Rachel is trying to say is we all feel like you're the perfect pup for the job. We all have to try new things and spread our wings."

Mackie flapped his newly earned wings. "Well, if you all think I should do it … then count me in. I'm your dog!" Mackie exclaimed.

Happy barking and yapping could be heard all over heaven that day! My oh my, what a lot of fur was flying. A lot of furry tails were wagging.

That was Mr. Mackie's introduction to heaven …

 … And the rest of the "tail" follows.

Choir Practice

"Welcome, furry friends," Mr. Mackie said. "I'm really feeling right at home. My bed is so comfy, the food is the best, and the air is sooooo sweet. I'm surrounded with a feeling of warmth and comfort, and mostly *love.* It inspires me.

"Thank you so much for having the confidence in me to elect me as your choir director. We'll make this a show that everyone remembers in their hearts forever."

Mackie hesitated for a minute, and then asked, "What shall we sing? Does anyone have any ideas or suggestions?"

The others sat contentedly in their hind-quarter-down positions and pondered what Mr. Mackie had asked. Precious finally piped up and said, "I would like to sing a solo."

"Typical," howled Sug One. "She always wants to be the center of attention!"

The gracious collie Rachel just shook her head.

"I mean really!" Muffy One exclaimed. "Sug doesn't even know Presh Dog. Other than noticing that Presh makes sure her bow in her hair is just right, she seems very nice. And she's really got quite a voice."

"Okay, pipe down, pups. How about I choose a couple of songs and we all just sing along? I think that things will just fall into place as they were meant to be," Mr. Mackie suggested.

As Mackie led the group in song, he noticed that they all were smiling and singing in unison. They all made such a beautiful sound.

Mr. Mackie looked around him and noticed that other animal friends were coming from numerous directions to see what all of the excitement was about. There were horses and bears approaching from the west, elephants, monkeys, lions, and tigers from the east.

Beautiful birds of all types were flying in, and there were sea animals: whales, dolphins, and fishies, in beautiful colors. All of them were popping their heads out of the meadow lake to see what was going on. Oh, what a joyous sight!

The doggies were very happy and proud that the other animals had come to hear them sing! As they enjoyed this special moment, they noticed that there were also people standing around the banks of Lake Dogdom.

Yes, humans, with huge smiling faces, clapping their hands and singing along with the choir.

It was a glorious sight to see!

"What a magnificent job you all have done!" Mr. Mackie exclaimed. "Now let's take a break for the day and join all of our new friends and get to know them. Give them the Dogdom welcome. Invite them into your home and share with them what you have, your home and food, your music, and above all, your love.

We'll meet back here tomorrow and we'll share stories of what you've learned from your new friends that are different from you. I really think it will inspire our program; at our next choir practice, we'll all share stories of what we've learned. Go now and have fun."

All the doggies sprinted off in different directions to introduce themselves to the furry and non-furry people that had come from all over heaven to fellowship with them.

Awakening

"Oh, what a great day in Dogdom—blue sky and sunshine. Is it like this every day?" Mackie wondered.

He stretched his furry front legs, raised his tail in the air, and looked about. All was quiet in Dogdom. "Could I be the first one up? Highly unlikely," he said with a yawn.

Ms. Rachel, the collie, walked up beside Mackie and licked him square in the middle of his tiny forehead with her big collie tongue. "Good morning, Mackie. Great choir practice last night!"

"Thank you, thank you, Ms. Rachel. By the way, your piano playing is excellent."

"Why thank you, Mr. Mackie," Ms. Rachel replied. "I hope the other furry people had a good time."

"I'm sure they did. I hope they have some interesting 'furry tails' to share with us today."

"Good morning, y'all," greeted Precious as she pranced toward them. "You will not believe who I met last night."

"Tell us, tell us!" Rachel arfed.

"Wait," Mackie piped in. "Presh, let's wait until choir practice and you can tell everyone your story."

Everyone showed up for choir practice that evening right on time. Mr. Mackie took his spot behind the podium and tapped his baton to get their attention. "Thanks for coming, my furry friends; I'm very eager to hear about your 'tails' from last night. We'll take turns at every practice.

"Precious has asked to go first and is very excited to tell everyone about her new friend," Mr. Mackie said. "So Presh, bark on."

Precious regally wagged her tail as she made her way to the podium. "Thank you," Presh arfed dramatically, "for allowing me this much-awaited time to recall this amazing story."

"Uh … Presh," Mackie interrupted, "will you tell us who you met?"

"Well, uh … okay," Presh sighed. "I'll try to be brief. Last night after choir practice, I met this really cool elephant from Africa. Her name is Kumba and she is really, really big! She weighs four tons."

The furry friends gasped! Whoa!

"Forget the bigness. Kumba is very gentle and kind too. She picked me up—way, way up—and set me on her back. I sort of got woozy, but it was fun. I could see a lot of things from up there. I felt like a princess! Actually," Presh gushed, "I am a princess! My pedigree declares that …"

"Oh dear, not again," barked Ms. Rachel.

"Stay on track, Presh. We don't need your pedigree here. Everyone is equal," Mr. Mackie encouraged.

"What does she eat? Not dogs, I hope!" chimed Sarg.

"She eats mainly fruit, leaves, grass, and roots from trees," Presh answered.

"What a relief," said Sarg.

"Kumba drinks forty gallons of water a day."

"That's got to be some kind of a record!" exclaimed Mr. Mackie.

Presh answered, "No sir, that's just normal for the African elephant."

"Amazing!" the choir chimed in harmony.

"She's got wrinkles," Sarg spoke up. "Is she old?"

"She's seventy," Presh replied. "That might be old in dog years, but elephants live and walk the earth a lot longer than we do. But that's not why she has wrinkles. Her thick skin and wrinkles protect her from the sun and keep her cool.

"Kumba told me that she stands almost all day and rarely sleeps, only catching a few winks before the sun rises. Definitely *not* a dog's life.

"Oh, and before I forget," Precious added, "elephants never forget! They remember their watering holes, trails, their friends and family members always and forever."

"Neato!" the choir said at once.

"Yes, yes, it is very neato," Presh gushed. "Kumba is kind, lively, strong-willed, mighty, and she's my friend."

Presh, finally at a loss for words, looked at Mr. Mackie.

Mackie looked toward the back of the sanctuary where the mighty elephant stood, and asked Kumba to join the choir. The mighty elephant stood strong and proud and lifted her trunk to the air and gave a hearty roar! All the dogs barked with joy!

Oh, what a great day in Dogdom! A day everyone can enjoy. And then Presh sang her solo. Again, all of God's creations came to see and hear what was going on.

And another "tail" awaits us all!